THE DOLL

A Horror Novella

SAVANNAH HOPF
G. MICHAEL HOPF

ISBN 13: 978-1-702448-34-5

Printed in the United States of America

To my Family

PROLOGUE

LEONARDTOWN, MARYLAND
MAY 7, 1878

The smell of smoke woke ten-year-old Sarah from a deep sleep. She shot up and looked around her dimly lit room, the only light coming from a kerosene lamp still burning on her nightstand.

In the hallway, outside her room, the patter of small feet echoed.

Sarah tossed aside her sheet and blanket, slid out of bed and into a pair of slippers on the floor.

The smell of smoke grew, causing her to become very alarmed.

She leaned over and turned the wick up on the lamp.

Light splashed across her room.

She rushed to the door, grabbed the knob, but paused when she again heard the faint patter of feet on the hardwood floor in the hall. "Mommy!" she cried out. A lump formed in her throat, and her stomach tightened as her instincts told her something was terribly wrong. "Mommy!" she hollered.

The footfalls stopped.

Sarah threw open the door.

Thick smoke billowed into her room, and the light from her lantern cast out into the darkened hallway and down on her doll Mary, which lay in the center of the hall.

"What are you doing here?" she asked. She moved toward Mary but stopped when she saw smoke pouring from underneath her parents' bedroom door. Fearful, she ran to their door and pounded on it with her small fists. "Mommy, Daddy!" The door felt warm to her touch. She grabbed the knob but recoiled when she found it was searing hot. "Mommy, Daddy!" she wailed. Terror gripped her. She needed to reach them, but she couldn't.

She coughed and wheezed as the heavy smoke began to take its toll on her. "Mommy, open up, Daddy!" She looked down and saw something wet on the floor. She knelt, touched it, and brought her hand to her face, only to recoil when she saw it was blood. It was then that she noticed a trail of it led to Mary. Confused, Sarah muttered, "Did you...no, you couldn't have."

Vertigo now gripped Sarah, her head swooned, and her ability to breathe was greatly reduced. She knew without a doubt her parents were gone, and if she didn't get out of the house, she would be too. Using all her strength, she crawled towards the stairs. As she passed Mary, she glanced and saw the doll was covered in blood. This confused her more. How could that be? How could Mary be in the hallway? The last she'd seen her was in bed with her.

Loud voices called out from the main floor below.

"Up here," Sarah cried out. She inched to the top step, peered over, and saw a man coming towards her. She reached for him then passed out.

THE MUFFLED VOICE OF A WOMAN WAS ALL SHE could remember hearing first. Sarah opened her stinging eyes for a second then closed them when the bright light of the sun hit them.

"The poor little dear is awake," the woman, who

Sarah knew as Mrs. Cunningham, said. "You just lie down, you hear."

"My parents?" Sarah said weakly, though she already had an idea of what their fate was.

Mrs. Cunningham turned to Doc Harris, a towering figure with long lanky arms, and said, "How about you let me tell the poor thing?"

Doc Harris snapped his satchel closed, gave Mrs. Cunningham a nod, and promptly left the room, closing the door behind him.

The bed creaked when Mrs. Cunningham sat on the edge of it. She took Sarah's hand, and just before she could open her mouth to speak, Sarah interrupted her.

"They're dead, aren't they?"

Making the sign of the cross, Mrs. Cunningham replied, "Yes, they are. They're with God now."

Tears filled Sarah's already painful eyes.

"You'll be fine, dear. We'll take care of you until we can get word to any relatives," Mrs. Cunningham said softly. "Oh, that reminds me. We found something that will warm your heart." She hopped up and rushed out of the room, only to return in seconds holding Mary.

The second Sarah laid eyes on the doll, she cried out, "No, no, not her, no!"

Stopped in her tracks by Sarah's response to the

doll, Mrs. Cunningham asked, "This is your doll, isn't it?"

"She did it. The doll did it!" Sarah screamed, her finger jabbing at it in the air.

Shocked, Mrs. Cunningham stepped back and furrowed her brow. "You're saying a simple wooden doll set fire to your house?"

"She did it. She did it!" Sarah wailed, her tone going from fear to frenzy.

"Calm down," Mrs. Cunningham snapped.

Doc Harris raced into the room. He went up to Sarah and pinned her down. "Get that thing out of here. It's upsetting her."

Mrs. Cunningham looked at Mary and shrugged her shoulders. "Looks like a nice enough doll. I'll go clean her up." She turned and exited the bedroom, leaving Doc Harris to handle Sarah's outburst.

"She did it! The doll did it! Mary killed my parents!" Sarah bellowed repeatedly.

I

NINE YEARS LATER

BALTIMORE, MARYLAND
OCTOBER 15, 1887

Unable to focus on her studies, Elizabeth or Lizzie as she liked to be called, watched the oil lamp's orange flame dance and cast bouncing shadows across her walls.

Today was her eighth birthday, not a significant one, like ten or thirteen, but to her, every birthday was an occasion to celebrate, especially since this would be the first birthday since her mother had died.

Soon her father, James, would be closing his cobbler shop, which conveniently was located in the basement of their three-story walk-up. She loved when he'd come upstairs from work. Like clockwork, he'd step into the hall, close the door, and call out her name in his deep baritone voice. Upon hearing him, she'd race from her upstairs bedroom, swoop down the wide stairs, and jump into his warm embrace. He'd wrap his trunk-like arms around her, give her a slight squeeze, and say softly, "I love you, Lizzy." What made tonight more exciting and different was, after he'd call her name, he'd add that he had a surprise for her.

Lizzie grunted when she looked at the ticking clock on the wall. She placed her pencil down and with a tone of frustration said, "Oh, hurry up." But what did she expect? She had only looked at the clock a minute before.

Thoughts of this expected surprise gift raced through her mind. *What will it be? Is it a wooden horse? I told him I wanted one. Maybe a toy drum? I mentioned I liked the one the boy had in the parade.* The need to know was making her anxious. She stood up and began to pace her room. Each step she took across the creaking wood floor counted for a second closer to her father arriving and the gift being presented.

A door slammed below.

She froze and listened, waiting for her cue.

"Lizzy, I'm home, and I have a surprise!" her father hollered.

Those words were music to her ears. She dashed from her room, ran down the stairs and, like every night, leapt into his arms. "Hi, Father!"

He hugged her and said, "I love you, Lizzy." He put her down and continued, "Go into the parlor. I have a surprise for you."

She sprinted down the hall and into the ornately decorated room. Her eyes darted back and forth until they spotted the one thing that was out of place. On the chaise lounge a long object sat wrapped in the thin sheets of the *Baltimore Sun* newspaper. *What can it be?* she asked herself. By the shape, it clearly wasn't a horse or a drum. She cautiously approached it.

He stepped into the room and watched with glee as she made her way to the gift. "Don't worry, it won't bite."

She laughed and said, "I just thought..."

He folded his arms and asked, "Thought what, sweetheart?"

"That it was something else," she said, now standing above the gift.

"Well, I hope you're not disappointed," he said.

She looked at him and asked, "Can I open it?"

"Of course, it's yours," he replied happily.

Just feet from her, the fire crackled and popped.

She sat next to the gift and went to grab it but hesitated. Thoughts of her last birthday and her now deceased mother washed over her.

Seeing her hesitation, he asked, "What's wrong?"

She lowered her head and answered, "I was just thinking about Mother. I miss her."

With a frown, he said, "I miss her too, sweetheart." He went to her side and sat down. Taking her hand, he continued, "Tonight is a time to celebrate and be happy. Your mother wouldn't want you sad right now."

"I know, I just...I just remember her sitting right there last year. I can't believe she's gone," she said, pointing to a large wingback chair across from them.

"Lizzy, go ahead, open your gift. Enjoy this moment. It's your day," he said.

She picked up the gift. It was heavier than she thought it would be. Her small fingers found the edge of the paper, but just before she tore, she again paused.

He put his arm over her shoulders and with a reassuring voice said, "Open it. Remember what your mother told you just before she went to God."

She looked into his eyes and answered, "I remember."

"What was it?"

"She said, life is for the living."

"That's right, now please open the gift. I know you're going to love it," he said.

Putting aside her melancholy thoughts, she slid her fingers under the edge and tore a large piece of paper away. It was enough to expose what hid inside.

"It's a doll," she exclaimed, ripping the remaining paper away and freeing the doll's slender arms and legs.

"It is. Do you like it?"

She examined the doll like a doctor would a new patient, her eyes diligently taking in every detail. From the black hair, rose-colored cheeks and pink lips, her examination stopped on the doll's eyes. "They're so blue, like the ocean."

"They're like your eyes," he said.

"He said the doll is an antique."

"It's old?" Lizzie asked, confused, as it looked so clean and new.

"Don't be disappointed. I've had a tough month and—"

"I love her," Lizzie said, interrupting him. She knew they had been having money troubles and was truly fine with the gift.

"You really love it?" he asked.

"I do. I love it. She's beautiful."

"You do?"

SAVANNAH HOPF & G. MICHAEL HOPF

"Yes, yes, I do," she replied and gave him a hug.

"Happy birthday, Lizzy," he said, returning the embrace. "Oh, the doll has a name, the man said."

Pulling away from him, she looked at the doll with curiosity and asked, "What is it?"

"Mary."

She held her up high and said loudly, "Nice to make your acquaintance, Mary."

2

BALTIMORE, MARYLAND
OCTOBER 16, 1887

With a hairbrush in hand and Mary on her lap, Lizzie sang a nursery rhyme her mother used to sing as she ran the brush through Mary's thick black hair.

"One, two, three, four, five. Once I caught a fish alive. Six, seven, eight, nine, ten, then I let it go again." She stopped brushing, leaned in and asked with a big smile stretched across her tender face, "Did you say something?"

Lizzie looked in the mirror at their reflection and again asked, "I swore I heard you say something. But that would be silly. You're just a doll made from wood. However, I do believe in magic, which means that you could, I suppose."

Humming loudly, Lizzie went back to brushing Mary's hair.

"Lizzie, it's suppertime," James hollered from below.

Again Lizzie glanced at Mary in the mirror. "Are you hungry? I know I am. Come, let's see what Father prepared for us." Lizzie put the brush down and hopped up from the chair, ensuring to keep Mary as steady as she could.

Mary was a larger doll than Lizzie was used to. Her two other dolls were much smaller and both made from a rough canvas and stuffed with fragments of linen with buttons for eyes. Mary was made of wood; her elbows and knees were actual joints with a bolt and nut. Her face was carved from a much larger block and smoothed to perfection with lacquer to seal it, then paint to cover. Her hair was an obsidian color, felt real to the touch, and was secured to the top of her head with glue. Standing around three feet, Mary was tall for Lizzie, who herself only towered six inches above that. Being that she was made of wood, she was heavy; yet Lizzie didn't flinch or complain anytime she carried her.

Down the stairs she raced with Mary in her arms.

She hit the ground floor, turned left and headed for the dining room, to find the table empty. She promptly went to her spot, pulled out the chair next to her, and sat Mary in it. "There you go." She pulled her chair back and plopped down. "Oh, let me get your napkin," Lizzie said to Mary, pulling the cloth napkin from underneath the silverware, and spread it across Mary's lap. "There."

The door that separated the kitchen and dining room swung open, and in came James holding a serving platter. He placed it on the table. Steam rose from the cut of meat and potatoes that accompanied it. "I got this roast on sale. Looks good," he said with a smile. "Oh, I see Mary joined us."

"Of course she did. She's one of the family," Lizzie said.

James cut some meat and placed it on Lizzie's plate along with a couple of small red potatoes. He served himself and asked, "Shall we say grace?"

"What about Mary? She needs some food," Lizzie protested.

James gave her a grin and said, "Shall we lower our heads in prayer?"

"But Mary," Lizzie grunted.

He shot her a look and said, "You can't be serious, Lizzie, she's a doll. I'm not going to waste good food to put on her plate."

"She's part of the family," Lizzie complained.

"She very well may be, but last I checked, she doesn't eat. Now lower your head and let's say grace."

Knowing her limitations when it came to her father, Lizzie didn't press.

He said grace and the two began to eat. Halfway through, he wiped his mouth and said, "I have an announcement to make."

"Am I to get a puppy?" she blurted out.

"No puppy, sorry. I wanted to let you know that I have a nice woman coming over to watch you tomorrow night, as I'm going out to dinner."

"Going out to dinner? With who?"

"I haven't said anything to you yet, but I met a very nice woman. I'm taking her to—"

"Woman? Who is this woman? Is she to be my mother?" Lizzie snapped.

"I haven't said that. I'm just going out with her tomorrow. She's a widow and—"

"Does she have children? What will become of me?" Lizzie asked, her previous tone of shock shifting towards sadness.

"Become of you? Oh my, no, no, no," he said and reached his hand across the table to take hers.

She recoiled. "Who is she?"

"She's a very nice woman. I've known her for a

month now. We've only gone for a walk and had tea. I'm taking her to dinner because—"

Again Lizzie interrupted him. "Are you going to ask her to marry you?"

"I, um..."

"You are. Did you not think about how I felt about this?" Lizzie barked.

"Lizzie, I didn't think I needed to get the permission of an eight-year-old," he fired back.

Tears broke free from Lizzie's eyes and streamed down her face. "Mother hasn't been dead for a year and you're ready to remarry?"

"I, um..." he muttered, unable to get a word in edgewise as Lizzie continued her verbal barrage.

"And she has children..."

"No, no, she doesn't. I only said she was a widow, nothing more."

"Still, I'm to now become second fiddle," Lizzie cried out. She stood up abruptly; her chair fell back and hit the wall. She snatched Mary from her chair and marched towards the hall.

"Lizzie Marie, you come back this instant, sit down, and finish your supper."

"Save it for your new wife!" Lizzie barked.

He got up from the table, raced towards her, but she was too fast. Up the stairs she flew, tears falling from her cheeks and chin.

"Lizzie, please!" he hollered; regret filled his words.

She ignored him, entered her room and slammed the door. She jumped on the bed and sobbed. She rolled onto her side, looked at Mary and groaned, "At least I have you."

A voice sounded, as if it were carried on a slight breeze.

Alarmed, Lizzie leaned in and asked, "Did you say something?"

Again a voice sounded. Like before, it was faint, almost inaudible.

Lizzie leaned in close to Mary and put her ear close. Her eyes widened when she heard something that was intelligible. "You do talk, but how?" She listened more intently, but the sounds were gone. She leaned back and looked carefully at Mary in disbelief. She was young and impressionable, but thinking that a doll could talk was something she just couldn't believe. She sighed and rolled onto her back, her eyes fixed on the white plaster ceiling. "I wish you were real. You could help me stop my father from marrying whoever this woman is."

3

BALTIMORE, MARYLAND
OCTOBER 17, 1887

The strong odor of mothballs washed over Lizzie as she cleared out a spot in the tall wardrobe. "This is a perfect hiding spot for you." With Mary in her right hand, she slid the doll into the back corner and went to close the door. But before she could, she heard a small voice just above a whisper sound all around her. Lizzie froze, unsure of what she heard. "Who's talking?" she asked out loud, though she knew no one was there. She glanced over her shoulder but found no one there, yet she heard what sounded like murmuring coming from all around her. She peered into the wardrobe. "Is that you, Mary?"

The doll sat motionless. Not a sound emanated from it.

With a furrowed brow, Lizzie stared at Mary. "Hmm." She pulled her head out of the wardrobe, only to have the sounds disappear. Thinking she must have misheard, she closed the wardrobe door and raced off to go count to twenty, her usual number when playing hide-and-seek.

"Eighteen, nineteen, twenty—ready or not, here I come," Lizzie said and ran into the spare room. She played along as she looked under the bed, in drawers of the dresser, and behind the door. "Where are you?" she asked out loud as she meandered to the wardrobe. "Are you in there?" she asked, a playful smile on her face, and her gaze upon the dark cherry wood door of the wardrobe.

Impatient, she threw open the door, but the doll wasn't there. "Mary?" She rummaged through the items but couldn't find the doll. "Mary, where are you?" she asked, confused about the doll being missing. All she could figure was her father must have found it. She spun around and tore out of the room. "Father!" she cried out as she bolted down the stairs.

"Father!" she again called out. From room to room she went looking for her father and the doll but found neither.

Voices carried from down in the basement. She opened the door that led there and heard her father's distinct voice as well as another man's. Curious as to where he'd taken Mary, Lizzie went down into his shop.

Catching sight of Lizzie out of the corner of his eye, James stopped talking to the man and turned. "I'm working, Lizzie."

"Sorry, Father, I'm looking for Mary."

"I don't know where your doll is. Now if you will excuse me."

"But you took her," Lizzie said.

The customer chuckled. "Best give your girl her doll."

A frown on his face, James snapped, "I didn't take your doll, Lizzie. Now please go back upstairs. I have a customer here."

"But where's Mary?"

"I don't know, Lizzie, now go!"

Upset, Lizzie sulked as she stomped her way back to the main level. She couldn't understand where Mary could have gone. Turning left, she walked towards the front door, but as she passed the parlor, she spotted Mary sitting in the bay window. Shocked, she ran over, a perplexed look on her face. "How did you get here?" She had looked in the parlor just before going down to her father's shop and could swear she hadn't seen her.

The doll sat, her blue-painted eyes focused on the street below.

Lizzie snatched Mary from her spot and held her. She looked into Mary's face and asked, "How did you get here?"

As if expecting to get a response, Lizzie waited.

She cradled the doll and said, "Let's go back to the wardrobe and play again." She ran to the stairs but stopped when she again heard the murmuring. Lizzie halted, looked down at Mary and asked, "Did you just say you're scared of the dark?" A murmur sounded, but it was unintelligible and it seemed to be coming from all around her as if it were floating or disembodied.

"Are you making those sounds?" Lizzie asked with a combination of excitement and fear. "Did you say you're afraid of the dark? I could swear that's what I heard." After a long pause, she said, "Let's play tea instead." With Mary in a warm embrace, she headed back up to her bedroom.

"Now, make sure she's in bed by seven, okay?" James said to the nanny.

"I can assure you, Mr. Wilkins, your lovely daughter will be in bed, eyes closed by then. I've been watching over little ones since I was seventeen," the nanny said with a crooked smile. She was an older woman, about sixty-three, heavy, and had a round rosy face. Her silver hair was pulled back into a tight bun.

"Then it appears I'll be leaving Lizzie in good hands, thank you. I'll return about eight," James said as he slid into his topcoat. He grabbed his bowler hat and cane and headed for the door, where Lizzie stood, Mary held close. "You listen to her, and be to bed when she says."

"Yes, Father."

He bent down and gave her a kiss on the cheek.

"Do you have to go?" Lizzie asked.

"I do, and you and I will talk more about this tomorrow, I promise." He donned his hat, threw open the door, and disappeared into the night.

When the door closed, the nanny cried out, "How about some warm milk and a cookie."

Lizzie cocked her head, shocked by the instant display of kindness, and asked, "Cookies? We don't have any."

The nanny walked to her purse, a large black leather bag, opened it, reached in and pulled out a small paper bag. "But I do. Now show me wear the kitchen is."

Not hesitating, Lizzie took her by the hand and escorted her to the kitchen.

❧

Lizzie found the nanny very sweet and pleasant, so much so that she hadn't given any attention to Mary.

"What's your favorite game?" the nanny asked.

"Hide-and-seek," Lizzie replied happily.

"Oh my, it's mine too," the nanny said, clapping with joy. "How about you go hide and I count?"

"Okay, but give me twice as much time so I can hide Mary too. She plays as well," Lizzie said.

Giving Mary a quick glance, the nanny paused; she couldn't explain it then, but the doll gave her the creeps.

"Go over there and count to forty," Lizzie said, pointing to the kitchen corner.

"Fine," the nanny said. She got up, walked to the corner, and began her count. "One, two..."

With Mary in her arms, Lizzie sprinted out of the

room and down the hall. She had the perfect spot for Mary in the hall closet, while she'd hide behind the curtains in the parlor.

The nanny's voice carried down the hall. "Twenty-one, twenty-two."

Lizzie threw open the closet door and set Mary in there, among the odds and ends that had no real home in the house. She closed the door and headed towards her spot.

❧

"THIRTY-NINE, FORTY—READY OR NOT, HERE I come," the nanny cried out. She promptly walked from the kitchen and into the warm and bright glow of the gas lights, which were spaced every eight feet. "Let me see here, if I were a little girl, where would I hide?" She spotted the dining room, went in, and looked under the table. "Hmm, not there." She saw the hall closet just outside the dining room and went directly there. "If I were a little girl, this would be a good place to hide."

She knocked on the door and said, "If you're in there, I'm coming to get you." She turned the knob slowly, stepped back, and threw open the door.

To her fright it wasn't Lizzie, but Mary she found

standing with a brass-handled cane in her hands. The nanny gave Mary an odd but concerned look, as something seemed off.

Mary came alive, swung the cane, and struck the nanny in the forehead.

The nanny wailed in pain, stumbled backwards, and fell to the floor. She looked up, only to see the doll take a step towards her. Filled with terror, the nanny jumped to her feet and screamed. She raced to the front door, threw it open and, without even grabbing her belongings, escaped into the dark of night, her screams echoing down the dimly lit street.

Confused and scared by what she'd heard, Lizzie emerged from her hiding place. She stepped into the hall, looked left to see the front door wide open, the cool air of the early evening blowing in. She turned right and saw the closet door ajar and the cane on the floor. She went to the closet and opened it fully to see Mary exactly where she'd left her. She picked up the cane and saw a small amount of blood on the handle, then again looked towards the front door with a growing sense of dread.

✦

"HELLO?" JAMES CALLED OUT UPON RETURNING home to find the nanny wasn't anywhere to be found.

He immediately went to Lizzie's room, opened the door, and saw through the soft glow of the lamp that she was there with Mary at her side. He stepped farther into the room, bent down to give her a kiss; but before he could, Lizzie opened her eyes.

"She left me," Lizzie said.

"The nanny?"

"Yes."

"When?"

"An hour after you left. She got scared when we were playing hide-and-seek. She ran off, leaving her belongings here."

"Are you okay?"

"I'm fine. I had Mary to keep me safe," Lizzie said, squeezing Mary.

"I'm so sorry. I'll have a word with her in the morning. I'll make sure she never works anywhere again," James said, gave Lizzie a peck on the cheek, and headed out.

"Goodnight," Lizzie said.

He stopped just outside the door. "Goodnight, Lizzie."

"Father," she said.

"Yes."

"Please don't leave me again," Lizzie urged.

Filled with regret about what had happened, he said, "I won't."

"Promise me."

"I promise," he replied and closed the door.

❧ 4 ❦

BALTIMORE, MARYLAND
OCTOBER 18, 1887

"Now sit here like you do every day and enjoy the view. I'll be home as quick as I can," Lizzie said as she sat Mary in the large bay window that overlooked the bustling city street below.

"I'm sorry I can't walk you today, Lizzie. I have a customer coming by who is promising. He might need me to provide care for all his workers' boots."

"That's good," Lizzie said. She walked to the front door, grabbed her slate and a sack that held her lunch. "I'm fine, I know the way. I could walk it blindfolded."

He bent down and kissed her on the forehead. "I'm really sorry about last night. I mean to contact the nanny later today. Also please be careful at the corner. You know how those grocery wagons like to race past."

"I'll be careful," Lizzie replied, a sweet and gentle smile stretched across her face.

James opened the door. A swift, cool, autumn breeze rushed in and brought with it a few dried leaves. "Brrr, stay warm."

"Bye-bye," Lizzie said with a wave. She headed down the steep front steps to the sidewalk. She gave her father one last look then turned to wave at Mary. "Bye, Mary."

"Best go. Don't want to be late," James said.

Happily and with a pep in her step, Lizzie marched down the street.

James watched until she cleared the busy intersection and disappeared around the corner a block farther. He closed the door, shivered at bit by how cold it was outside, and headed to the basement door. An odd feeling gripped him, making him stop just in the entryway to the parlor. Something told him that he was being watched. He slowly turned his head and looked in the parlor, fully expecting to see someone, but it was empty. He spotted Mary in the window, her face reflected in the glass. "Hmm, that's peculiar," he mused out loud. Ignoring the feeling, he pressed forward and went down to his shop.

❦

WITH A FIRM HANDSHAKE, HE SEALED A DEAL WITH Mr. Gaskin, the owner of the textile factory located near the inner harbor. Mr. Gaskin provided his workers shoes as a benefit, and in order to keep from replacing them, he was going to have many shoes in need of repair.

James followed Mr. Gaskin out. "I'll be ready to take any of your workers' shoes when you have them."

"Sounds good. Thank you for your time," Mr. Gaskin said, tipped his hat, and walked to a horse-drawn carriage that was waiting for him.

Filled with hope that business was turning around, James went back to his shop and, with a clenched fist, expressed his joy by holding his fist in the air and shouting, "Praise be." He pressed his eyes closed and saw him and Lizzie doing better, free of worry about their finances.

The patter of feet sounded above.

Torn from his thoughts, James opened his eyes and looked up.

More footfalls could be heard, these now near the door at the top of the stairs.

Curious if Lizzie might be home, he first looked at the clock on his wall and saw it was much too early unless she had come home due to illness. He rushed up the stairs, opened the door, and called out, "Lizzie, are you home?"

Silence.

He closed the door behind him and again called out, "Hello, Lizzie, are you home?"

Nothing but silence.

He looked at the front door and saw it was locked. He walked over just to double-check, and that was when he spotted that Mary was not at her perch in the bay window. Finding it odd, he again assumed it had to be Lizzie at home. He spun around, went to the base of the stairs, which led up to the second floor, and hollered, "Lizzie, this is not a time to play around. If you're home, reply."

No reply came.

A different sound came from the second floor. It wasn't footfalls. Nor did it sound like someone was moving; it sounded like many people whispering.

A tinge of fear rose in him. "Who's up there?"

The whispering grew.

Unsure what or whom he might encounter, he stepped back from the base of the stairs, went to the foyer, grabbed his favorite cane, and came back. "Whoever is up there, show yourself!"

The whispers again rose in volume.

"I'm armed and have every intention of defending myself and my home," he said and took a few steps up. "Come out and show yourself this instant!"

The patter of feet came from near Lizzie's bedroom.

"I hear you," he barked. Pushing his fear aside, he ran up the remaining stairs. When he put his foot on the landing, the whispers stopped. His eyes darted back from Lizzie's bedroom door, which was closed, to his across the hall from it. "I've warned you."

With determination, he went to Lizzie's door, grabbed the knob and quickly let go when he found it icy cold. He looked at his hand and flexed it. His instincts were telling him not to open the door, but his honor and duty as a man screamed at him to defend his house from the intruder. He took hold of the knob, ignoring the chill, turned it and pushed open the door.

Sitting on the edge of the bed was Mary, her wooden arms folded and lying on her lap.

James stared at the doll. Again his senses told him to flee, but he couldn't. "Whoever is here, come out!"

In his right hand, he gripped the came with a white-knuckle intensity. "I demand you come out!"

Defiant, he stood in the doorway, ready to do battle with whoever was there, but no one appeared. He looked around the room and glanced under the bed, but it was empty. Annoyed, he turned and went to his room. There he found no one. To the spare room—again, nothing. He checked every space he could and came up empty-handed. Confused, he went back to Lizzie's room, only to find Mary still sitting as he'd found her. He looked into her blue eyes and could feel someone staring back at him. When he thought about that, he dismissed the idea, as it seemed foolish to think the doll was really looking back. He began to question whether he'd heard anything or even correctly recalled Mary had been downstairs.

After a long pause, he pushed the thoughts out of his mind and chuckled that he could have even entertained the thought that the doll had walked itself upstairs.

"Lizzie must have left you here. I don't know why I thought otherwise," he said out loud, hoping to reassure himself. He had work to do, and this had proved to be a great distraction. He went back downstairs, headed to the foyer to drop off the cane, but hesitated from putting it away. Still not convinced completely, he kept the cane and went back to his shop.

SLAMMING THE DOOR BEHIND HER, LIZZIE ENTERED the foyer, stripped off her coat, scarf, and hat, and tossed her slate and book on the table. "I'm home, Mary!" she cried out in joy. She ran to the parlor, only to find Mary wasn't there. "Are we playing hide-and-seek already?"

Hearing her arrival, James went to greet her. "Hi, Lizzie."

"Have you seen Mary?" Lizzie asked.

"She's upstairs on your bed where you left her," he answered.

"I didn't leave her there. I left her there," Lizzie said and pointed at the bay window.

"No, you left her upstairs."

"No I didn't. I left her there," Lizzie countered.

"You're mistaken, because she's upstairs, sitting on your bed where you left her," James said, his hands firmly planted on his hips.

"I didn't leave her there," Lizzie again protested and walked off.

Shaking his head in confusion, he said, "Lizzie,

please stop. I have something else to discuss with you."

She did as he asked, spun around and looked at him.

"I have something for you, please, come," he said and walked into the parlor.

"Can I go get Mary?" she asked.

"No, now please come and sit down," he urged. His hand motioned to the chaise lounge.

She walked into the parlor, sat and smoothed out her skirt, which had gotten wrinkled.

He walked to a console table behind her, opened a drawer, pulled out a small box wrapped in brown paper, and came back. He held it in his hand and sat across from her. "Lizzie, I wanted to apologize for not being open about my feelings for, much less even mentioning, Miss Melody."

Lizzie didn't reply, her eyes giving him an emotionless stare.

"I should have understood your feelings in regard to this, and for that I'm truly sorry."

"Does this mean you won't be seeing her again?" she asked.

He sighed and looked at the box in his hands. "I got this for you as a token." He handed her the box.

Her eyes wide with curiosity at what it could be, she asked, "What is it?"

"Open it up and find out."

She tore through the paper and opened the small cardboard box to find a variety of chocolates.

"Something sweet for someone sweet." He smiled.

"Can I have one now?" she asked.

"Yes."

She picked one up and took a bite. As the sweet chocolate melted on her tongue, a smile began to spread. "Yummy."

"I think that's a yes, that they're good."

"Thank you," she said.

"You're welcome. Am I forgiven?"

She put the half-eaten chocolate back in the box, set it aside, and walked over. She touched his face and sat down next to him. "Of course I forgive you. I just can't imagine another woman being my mother. I had one and God took her from me."

Tears filled his eyes upon hearing her words.

She rested her head against his shoulder and said, "I love you, Father."

"And I love you."

"Can I go play with Mary now?"

"Yes, of course, and please be down for supper promptly at five thirty. We..." he said before cutting himself off.

She looked at him and asked, "We?"

"Just be cleaned up for supper then, okay?"

"Okay, Father," she said happily, got up, grabbed her chocolates, and raced away.

A heavy burden gripped him, as he hadn't been honest with her even while apologizing for just that.

"LIZZIE, COME TO SUPPER!" JAMES CALLED OUT.

Frantic, Lizzie grabbed Mary, threw open her door, and raced out. She rushed down the stairs and cried out, "I'm sorry, Father, I lost track of time." She hit the ground level and went into the dining room. "I'm..." she said, then froze upon seeing a beautiful young woman sitting in a chair next to her father's.

The woman, who was slight, standing about five feet two inches, with a lean frame, stood and said, "You must be Lizzie."

Lizzie shot her father a hard stare and asked, "Is this the woman?" Her tone displayed her confusion and anger.

James stood, returned Lizzie's hard stare, and said firmly, "Lizzie, this is Miss Melody Griffin. She is our guest tonight for supper."

"But you said—"

"I said nothing about her coming or that we'd still see each other, I merely apologized to you because I didn't inform you, and I'm still regretting that I hadn't been more forthright. Please sit down and show her the respect she deserves."

"But you, you told me today," Lizzie snapped.

"I apologized. I didn't say anything about not seeing her," he replied defensively. "Now, please take your seat."

Melody was rigid, and by her body language she felt very uncomfortable. "And who do you have there?" she asked, referring to Mary.

Ignoring her, Lizzie sat in her chair and sat Mary next to her.

James cleared his throat and said, "Lizzie, answer her question."

"Mary, her name is Mary."

"Hi, Mary, my name is Melody," she said sweetly before taking her seat.

"I'll be honest, I didn't make dinner tonight. I hired someone to do it," James said, he too sitting.

"That's so nice of you," Melody said. Her hand reached out and touched his.

Seeing the affection between the two, Lizzie grunted loudly.

"Lizzie, behave or you'll go to your room."

"The food smells delicious," Melody said, a grin on her face though she wasn't feeling happy about the reception she'd received so far. She turned to Lizzie and said, "Your house is very nice."

"I know, my mother decorated," Lizzie growled.

"Go to your room, now," James said, his tone stern.

Lizzie jumped up, grabbed Mary, and marched out of the room.

"Before you leave, apologize to Miss Melody."

Finding all her strength, Lizzie stopped, turned and faced Melody. "I apologize."

"Go, we'll discuss your behavior later," James said.

Not hesitating, Lizzie whisked up the stairs and into her room, slamming the door behind her.

"I should go too," Melody said.

"Heavens no, you're my guest, and I need to apologize for my daughter," James said. He went on to confess that he hadn't discussed her with Lizzie, and it was nothing but Lizzie dealing with the shock of him possibly loving someone else. He admitted his approach had been wrong, and now he was dealing with the ramifications of it.

The two enjoyed their supper and retired to the parlor for a drink.

"A brandy?" he asked after starting a fire.

"Sounds delightful," she said.

"I'll get one, but first I'll go up and check on Lizzie. Give me a moment," James said. He rushed upstairs and found Lizzie in bed, sleeping with Mary next to her. Confident that he and Melody would have some time to talk without Lizzie interrupting, he went back to the parlor.

He poured two glasses of brandy from a decanter and presented one to Melody.

"So your shop is downstairs?" Melody asked.

"It is, just below us. I'm fortunate that I get to work from my home," he said before taking a sip. "Do you want to see it?"

"I'd love to," she replied.

"I can assure you it's not as special as you think," he said, hoping to show his modesty.

"I need to take a bit of a break. Where do I go so I can..."

"I have indoor plumbing, just down the hall, left door before the kitchen."

"You have a water closet?"

"Yes, I have a bathing tub and sink as well," James said, prideful. "There's an oil lamp just inside on a table."

Excited about not having to go to use an outhouse, Melody excused herself. She walked the short distance down the hall and opened the door. The light from the hall illuminated the dark bathroom and enabled her to see the oil lamp exactly where he said it would be. She lit it and closed the door for privacy.

As he waited, James remembered that his shop

was a bit untidy. Not wanting to make a bad impression, he left to clean it up. The wooden steps creaked under his weight. He had forgotten to bring a light source, so he stepped into the dark. Knowing where an oil lamp was, he slowly walked to it. His foot hit something on the floor, then another thing. He found it odd, as nothing should have been in his way. He bent down and reached. The second his fingers touched it, he knew it was a shoe. "What are you doing there?" he asked out loud. He continued to his workbench, hitting other shoes that lay strewn on the floor. He lit the oil lamp, showering his shop in a warm orange glow and showing him the extent of disarray his shop was in. "How did this happen?" he asked. He picked up another shoe and found the upper had been sliced. He looked and saw most had been damaged, their leather uppers marred and cut. "Lizzie!" he bellowed. What made this worse was these were the shoes from his new contract.

Upstairs, Melody finished her business, washed her hands, and left the bathroom to find the hall dark, as the gas lamp on the wall was out. The only light came from the parlor fireplace.

The sound of footfalls came from in front of her.

"Is that you?" she asked, referring to James.

Unable to see, she took a couple of cautious steps, with her hands out in front of her.

The footfalls grew loud until they were in front of her.

Pain came from her left hand, causing her to recoil it. "Ouch." Then something hit her right arm, with a stinging pain coming from it. She cried out and pulled back from whoever was in front of her.

Down in his shop, James heard Melody. He dropped what he was doing and ran upstairs. He opened the door to find the hall darkened, but the sounds of Melody screaming came from his right. He went to the gas lamp and turned it up. The light washed over the hall and exposed splotches of blood on the hardwood floors. "Oh my," he gasped and ran to her.

Melody was on the floor, her back against the wall. Now able to see, she wailed at the sight of cuts on her left palm and right forearm.

He dropped to his knees and went to provide care.

"She cut me!"

"Lizzie did this?"

"Yes, she turned off the light, came down, and attacked me," Melody wailed as blood poured from her wounds.

"Let me get something to stop the bleeding and bandage you," he said and raced to the kitchen. He returned quickly and provided much-needed first aid, to find the wounds weren't deep and didn't require stitches. As he finished securing the last bandage, he said, "I don't know what to say, I'm truly sorry. This isn't like her. She's a sweet girl."

Angered, Melody held up her bandaged wounds and snapped, "Sweet girls don't do this." She got to her feet and made for the front door.

"Don't go. Please stay."

"No, I need to go."

"Let me walk you home," he said.

"I'll be fine. It's only a block and a half away."

"I know, but let me escort you home for safety," he pleaded.

"It's safer out there than in here," she cried out.

"I'll talk to her. I'm so sorry," he said and watched her walk towards her things near the front door in the foyer.

She grabbed her belongings, tossed open the door, and disappeared into the dark of night.

With Melody gone, quite possibly from his life, James' sorrow over the incident turned to anger. He slammed the door and marched up to Lizzie's room. Unconcerned, he burst into her room and yelled, "How dare you!"

Groggy from sleeping deeply and shocked by her father's sudden appearance, Lizzie sprang up, rubbed her eyes, and asked, "What's wrong?"

He turned up the lamp on her nightstand and again hollered, "How dare you!"

"What's wrong? What have I done?"

"You attacked Miss Melody. You cut her. Where's the knife?" he asked and went to searching her room.

"I cut her? I don't know what you're saying, but I haven't left my room since supper."

"You went downstairs and attacked her as she left the wash closet. I can't fathom this sort of thing from you, yet here we are. I know you're angry with me about not being honest, but to take your anger out on her, an innocent and decent woman, is...well, it's despicable. I don't know who you are."

Tears flowed from Lizzie's eyes as fear took control of her body. She didn't know how to respond to her father except to keep denying the accusation. "I didn't do it, Father, I swear. I've been asleep."

"You can't even be honest with me. Who else could have done this? Huh? The doll? Please, Lizzie, you can at least show some dignity by not lying to me."

"I didn't do it!" she bellowed, tears streaming down her flush cheeks.

"I should take my belt and whip you, but I promised your mother I'd never do such a thing, so I'm left with one thing, and that's taking everything of value from you. From now on you only go to school, and when you return, straight to your room. Once in your room, you'll stay here until supper. On weekends, you'll stay in your room with nothing, no books, no paper, no slate, no toys...including Mary, especially Mary," he said and moved towards the doll.

Lizzie snatched Mary and held her tight. "No!"

"Give her to me, Lizzie."

"Please, I did nothing. I was asleep. I didn't hurt her, I swear it!" Lizzie pleaded.

His anger reached its peak. No longer able to be patient, he violently tore Mary from Lizzie's grasp and scooped up her other belongings. "You'll get them back when you've proven you can be a good person."

"No, please, don't do this!" she begged.

"When you sleep tonight, know that your actions tonight, what you did to her, were beyond anything your mother would have expected from you. I haven't even mentioned what you did to those shoes in my shop. Do you realize you cost me—us—a lot of money tonight and quite possibly that contract?"

Confused, Lizzie asked, "Shoes? Father, I don't know anything about that. I've done nothing."

"You need to not only pray for God's forgiveness but to your mother in heaven." He turned and barged out of the room, slamming the door behind him.

Alone, fearful and confused, Lizzie wailed.

He heard her cries all the way in his shop. There he put Mary and the other toys in a trunk. Before he closed it, he felt something wet on his hand; he looked and saw blood. He then stared at Mary and saw she had a small amount on her wooden hands. With a raised brow, he gave the doll a hard stare and asked something he never thought he'd ask. "Did you hurt Melody?"

An odd silence fell over him. Unable to keep his eyes on the doll any longer, he slammed the trunk lid closed and walked off.

※ 5 ※

BALTIMORE, MARYLAND
OCTOBER 19, 1887

James heard his door creak open and the pitter-
patter of feet coming towards him. He lifted
his head, his eyes half open trying to see who it
was, but before he could see clearly, Lizzie
jumped on the bed.

"Thank you, Father," she said warmly, her left arm
around his neck.

Confused by her sweet sentiment, he pulled back
for a moment and asked, "Thank you for what?"

"For giving me Mary back," she said.

"Huh?" he asked, looking over her small body to

see the doll in her right arm. "Why did you go get the doll? I told you that I had taken it away until further notice."

"I didn't get the doll. I woke and she was in bed with me."

A chill ran down James' spine. Once more he didn't know what to make of the strange situation. It was impossible for a doll to move on its own, so it had to be Lizzie. "Why did you go get the doll without my permission?"

"I didn't. I woke and she was there. I thought you brought her back to me," Lizzie answered, her tone showing fear.

"Lizzie, you destroyed all those shoes, then you cut Melody, and now you go and take your doll back after I took it away. What am I supposed to do with you? Do you need to go see a doctor?" he asked, sitting up.

"Please don't take her away again. I need her," she pleaded and wrapped both arms tightly around the doll.

James looked at her with a tinge of anger, which quickly evaporated to sympathy. He loved her more than anything, and it didn't help that she looked a lot like her mother. "I'm at my wits' end. I don't know what to do with you." He put his hand to his face and sighed loudly.

"I'll be better, I promise. I won't speak badly about Miss Melody anymore."

"But you hurt her. You cut her with a knife," James stressed.

"Father, I didn't. I didn't do it."

He gave her a long look and asked, "If you didn't, who did? And who went into my shop and destroyed those shoes? Am I supposed to be looking for some sort of apparition?"

Lizzie went quiet and turned ashen. She put Mary down on the bed, leaned in close to James and, with her hand covering her mouth, whispered, "I think Mary did it."

"The doll?"

"Ssh," she said.

Playing along, he whispered, "You're telling me that doll walked down to my shop and did those things, then came up and attacked Melody?"

She nodded.

"Lizzie, it's a doll; dolls don't do things like that. Dolls can't move," he blared, unable to control his volume.

"She does."

The sensation of another presence in the room hit him. He looked around, then settled his gaze on Mary, whose head was cocked and facing him. "You truly think the doll did it?" he asked as a spine-tingling chill shot through him.

She again nodded then gave Mary a sheepish look. "Sorry."

He leaned in like she had been doing, and whispered, "What should we do about it?"

"I don't know, but she didn't mean it. She was only looking out for me. I promise she won't do it again," Lizzie said.

"You talk to the doll?" he asked, now curious if she was having some sort of detachment, which could explain her belief that she hadn't actually done anything.

"Not really talk, but she communicates with me," Lizzie replied.

Her response gave him goose bumps, but only because he was now theorizing that she was using the doll as a vehicle for her actions. "Can you describe it?"

"I hear voices, lots of them. I think they're coming from her."

"Lizzie, you know this sounds ridiculous, don't you?" he asked, challenging her.

"But it's true. I didn't hurt Miss Melody, it was Mary. I didn't go to your shop and do anything to those shoes, it had to be..." Lizzie said while motioning with her head to Mary.

James glanced at the clock on his dresser and said, "I need you to go get ready for school. We can continue this discussion later."

"Can I take her with me?"

"Yes, but she stays up in your room today. I don't want to see her down in the window."

Lizzie jumped into his embrace. "Thank you, thank you. I promise I'll talk to her about doing bad stuff."

"Lizzie, I love you."

"I love you too," she repeated. With Mary back in her grip, she hopped off the bed and ran for the door.

"And, Lizzie."

"Yes, Father."

He opened his mouth to say something but paused. He'd already gotten his point across, and it didn't make any sense to belabor it. "It's nothing. Go get ready."

"Okay," she said and rushed off.

He shook his head with disbelief. He had his suspicions about the doll, but his logical mind told him that dolls aren't alive and they especially don't go around cutting people or destroying things. He fell back into his down pillows, grunted and stared at the plaster ceiling. He questioned whether he was up to the task of raising a child on his own. Maybe her outburst and the violence she'd showed against

Melody were a result of his bad parenting. Whatever was wrong with her, he clearly needed to be more present in her life and be there even more than he was before. But he also knew that she needed to see someone professional, a doctor who could help diagnose what was happening and find a cure or a means to help her. His only hesitation was he didn't want her sent away, which they often would require. Torn as to what he should do, he settled on just doing more himself, with hopes that it would all go away.

WITH FLOWERS AS A TOKEN OFFERING, JAMES attempted to contact Melody but didn't make it past the threshold of the house where Melody rented a room. The woman she rented from took the flowers and, with an angry look, sternly told James she'd pass along the flowers, but that was it. She informed him that Melody would not be receiving further communication from him, and if he showed his face anywhere near her, she'd contact the police. This news disheartened him, but what could he expect? He returned home and went to cleaning up his shop and thinking about the other big issue he had, the shoes that had been destroyed.

The rest of the day went without any incident.

Lizzie returned home, but without the normal pep in her step. She went to her room and, upon being summoned for supper, came down without a reminder and without Mary.

"Where's Mary?" he asked.

"I left her. I wanted us to just have supper together," she said, her tone subdued. She took her seat and sat quietly.

He served her a roasted chicken leg and potatoes, one of her favorite meals; yet she didn't seem excited. "What vexes you?"

"I'm scared," she confessed.

Hearing her utter those words, he took her hand and asked, "What scares you?"

"I've told you that I didn't hurt Miss Melody, and I'm not lying when I say that. I know you don't believe me, and that makes me scared that you'll send me away to a hospital for crazy people."

"I would never do that."

"My friend Agatha said her aunt had some issues. Her father told her that her aunt wasn't quite right in the head, so they sent her to a hospital for people who are crazy."

"I would never send you away. Don't listen to stories like that from your friend," he said.

"But you said you might send me to see a doctor."

"I did say that, but I would never have you sent away, never, ever, I swear that to you."

"But you don't believe me. You think I did those horrible things," Lizzie said, tears in her eyes. She touched his hand and continued, "Daddy, I didn't do anything bad, I swear it. It was Mary."

"Not the doll excuse again. Lizzie, dolls are inanimate objects. They're not alive; they can't do anything."

"She can."

"No she can't."

"You even use a pronoun when referring to her, what does that say?"

"It says nothing," he replied with a sigh. "This is all my fault. I should never have kept my relationship with Melody secret. I didn't realize how much stress that was going to put on you. I'm very sorry, and I won't do it again."

"But—"

He raised his hand and said, "I know what you're going to say. I can assure you that it won't happen again."

"She seemed nice," Lizzie said.

"She is."

"I'm sorry I was mean to her, and I am sorry for what happened to her too," Lizzie said.

He liked her finally saying that she was sorry for

what happened. He took it as an admission, and for now that was good enough. "Let's eat before it gets cold."

The two ate, chatting about school, puppies, and the Christmas holiday, which would soon be upon them. After supper, she went to her room, while he retreated to the parlor for a brandy and a warm fire.

"LIZZIE!" THE WHISPERS SAID IN UNISON.

Lizzie woke; her eyes darted around the dimly lit room. She sat up, rubbed her eyes, and saw Mary sitting up facing her at the end of the bed.

"What are you doing down there?" Lizzie asked, fear rising in her.

The whispers started.

Lizzie's fear soon turned to terror. She held her hand over her ears to block out the various voices coming from all around her, but it did no good. "Please stop, please."

Her pleas went unheeded.

Able to make out what they said, Lizzie snapped back, "No, he's a good father. I love him. No, I won't hurt him, nor will you."

The whispers grew in volume.

On the verge of screaming, Lizzie held it in,

fearing any outburst from her would only bolster that she was crazy. She snatched Mary from the end of the bed, hopped out of bed, and went to her door.

Louder the whispers got.

"Stop it, please," Lizzie groaned. She turned the knob and threw open the door.

The second the door opened fully, the whispers ceased.

Lizzie gave Mary a look and said, "Thank you, but I can't sleep with you tonight, I'm sorry."

Down the stairs, Lizzie went; the glow of the fire in the parlor marked her destination. Timidly she entered the room to find her father relaxing, a brandy snifter in his hand.

"Yes," he said upon seeing her.

"I don't want to sleep with her tonight."

"You don't? But just this morning you were so happy to have her," he said, confused by her reversal.

"She scares me now. She keeps whispering to me," she said, holding out Mary for him to take.

He took the doll and set it on the floor next to his chair. "Come here."

She sat on his lap, the fire warming her.

"What do you mean she whispers to you?" he asked, genuinely curious. This was the second time she'd mentioned it, and he did recall also hearing something that sounded like whispers the other day.

"I hear whispers all around when she's in the room. At first I thought it was fun, but now I'm scared."

"What scares you about it?" he asked, not sure if he should believe her, but then again he'd had his own experience, one that he didn't want to completely admit was real.

"She doesn't like you," Lizzie confessed.

He chuckled, gave Mary a glance, and asked, "You don't like me, huh?"

"It's not funny. I think she might try to hurt you," Lizzie said.

Hearing enough, he got firm and said, "Lizzie, you're taking this a bit far. It's just a doll made from wood, nothing more." He picked Mary up, pulled off parts of her clothes, and knocked on her torso with his knuckles. "Hear that? Just wood, nothing more."

"But she whispers to me, and I think she moves around too. Even you must think that. I did leave her in the window the other day, and when I came home, she was in my room."

Getting scared himself, he resisted the notion that the doll was alive and malevolent. "Lizzie, listen to yourself. This is nonsense. The doll is nothing but wood, paint, glue, bolts, etcetera."

"But—"

"No more buts, she can stay down here, but

59

please stop with these stories and make-believe fantasies. You're scaring yourself."

Her face drew long. "I'm going to go back to bed."

"Goodnight," he said, watching her saunter out of the parlor. "I love you."

"Love you," she whimpered and disappeared.

He picked up his snifter, swirled the brandy inside, and took a sip. He again glanced at Mary. A chill shot through him. Although he'd had his own odd experiences with the doll, admitting that it was alive was a bit too far for him to go. He grabbed Mary by the arm, picked her up, and walked to the bench on the far wall. He lifted the lid of it and dropped Mary inside. "I don't like you either," he said and closed the lid.

A knock on the door came just at that moment and startled him. He shot a look to the clock on the mantel and saw it was close to nine thirty, late for anyone to come solicit. He then thought it could be Melody and rushed to the front door. He unlocked the door and opened it quickly, hoping she'd be standing there, but it wasn't her; instead it was another woman, younger, and all in black.

"Mr. Wilkins?" the woman asked from behind a black veil.

"Who is asking?"

"My name is Sarah, and I have something urgent

to discuss with you."

"Urgent, is it about Melody?"

Sarah lifted her veil. "No."

"Then what does this urgent matter concern at this late hour?"

"It concerns your daughter."

"Has something occurred at school?"

"Mr. Wilkins, there's a chill in the air. May I come in? I can assure you that what I have to tell you is life or death."

James' brow furrowed. "Life or death?"

"Yes."

"Come in," he said and stepped aside.

Sarah stepped across the threshold. She looked around the house then froze. "Where is she?"

"My daughter is—"

"No, where's Mary?"

James closed the door and, with a perplexed look stretched across his face, stepped in front of Sarah and asked, "Mary the doll?"

"Where is she?"

"Miss?"

"Just call me Sarah."

"Sarah, who gave you my information? Was it the store?"

"Yes. Mr. Wilkins, the doll is evil. I need to take it away from here. It must be destroyed."

Shocked, James held up his hands, palms out, and said, "The doll is evil? Miss...Sarah, it's a doll, just wood and other stuff. This talk, first my daughter, now—"

"Your daughter knows?"

"She told me the doll hurt someone, someone close to me, and now she says she's scared of it. I have it stored in the bench over there," he said and pointed to the parlor.

Sarah bolted past him and towards the parlor.

"Wait, you can't just go where you like. This is my house," James said as he pursued her.

Sarah made it to the bench, lifted the lid, and gasped when she set her eyes on Mary. "You."

Looking down, James saw the doll was in the same position as when he tossed her in the bench. "This is just ridiculous, you know that," James said as goose bumps dotted his skin. His pragmatic and practical mind was at war with his instincts.

She reached for Mary, but he stopped her. "You're not going to take my Lizzie's doll."

"But she must be destroyed, you don't understand. She killed my parents. She's killed many more."

"Miss...sorry, Sarah, I think I need you to leave. This hocus-pocus and conjuring of demons or whatever you think is going on with this doll is, is just... well, it's nonsense."

"You've had experiences too, haven't you?" she asked.

"Ahh, odd, but it was just my imagination."

"Have you heard the whispers?"

Fear rose in him, but again he pushed it back, as he couldn't allow himself to believe. "Sarah, I need you to leave. I'm sorry about what happened to your parents, but this doll hasn't done a thing. It's just wood, nothing more."

"The doll is wood, and that wood came from the very tree the witches in Salem were hanged from over almost two hundred years ago."

"Now you're talking about witches and Salem? Everyone who has their wits and half a brain knows those poor people who were killed weren't witches. What happened in Salem was a crime and happens when people believe in ghouls and superstitions."

"It's real, Mr. Wilkins. It's real and that doll embodies the soul of a witch who is here to destroy whomever it belongs to."

James thrust his arm up, pointed at the door, and barked, "Leave now. I've asked nicely, but now I must insist strongly."

"Mr. Wilkins, please, I beg you, let me free you of this evil. She must be destroyed," Sarah said, her fingers intertwined and hands clasped together as if in prayer.

"Out."

Not taking no, Sarah reached for Mary, but again, James stopped her by taking her arm; this time though he took a firm hold and pulled her towards the door. "It is time for you to take your leave." He opened the door and shoved her out. "Don't ever come back."

"Mr. Wilkins, please!"

"Go now before I summon the police."

"Your daughter, you are at risk. She is evil; she will not rest until she kills again."

"And I will be having a word with the proprietor of the toy store too. He will get an earful from me. How dare he give away my address," James said and slammed the door.

Sarah's muffled pleas could be heard on the other side of the door.

He pulled the drape away from a small side window and yelled, "Go away!"

She stayed for a few minutes longer to beg but eventually left.

Back in the parlor, his drink in hand, James stood above the still-open bench and stared at Mary. "I will say this about you, Mary; you definitely have an influence on people. But I won't be fooled that you're nothing more than just wood and paint." He shut the lid and went back to relaxing in his chair.

6

BALTIMORE, MARYLAND
OCTOBER 20, 1887

"Father, can I put Mary in the window this morning?" Lizzie asked.

"I thought you didn't like her anymore," James asked, his brow furrowed as once again Lizzie shifted her feelings about the doll.

"I said that she scared me...sometimes. I like seeing her in the window when I come and go to school," she clarified.

"Whatever you want to do, she's in the bench," James said, getting his coat on as he readied to walk her to school.

Without hesitation, Lizzie went to the bench. With her small hands she lifted the creaky lid. There, lying on top of a quilt, was Mary, just as she had been when James put her in there. Lizzie took her out. "Sorry my father put you in here, but I needed some alone time last night."

"Hurry, Lizzie, or we'll be late," James called from the foyer.

Lizzie rushed to the bay window and sat Mary in her spot. "I'll see you when I come home. Be a good girl." Lizzie met her father at the front door and the two exited. Out on the street, Lizzie gave Mary one last look. "I see you!" she said loudly and waved.

The two walked down the street, deep in conversation. What they hadn't noticed was Sarah hiding behind the corner of a house across the street.

Sarah waited until they were past the first intersection and out of sight before she made her move. She sprinted across the street and up the stairs. She tried the door, but it was locked. The hairs on her neck rose. She looked to her right and saw Mary in the window. "I'm coming to get you, you hear me." Frustrated that the door was locked, she made her way to the shop door below and found that too was locked. Determined to get inside, but without making herself noticed, she went to the back door, which was accessible off an alleyway. She first tried the knob, but like the others it was locked. A small window to her left was the only way. She pushed on it, hoping it would lift, but it wouldn't. Undeterred, she found a brick and threw it through, smashing the window into hundreds of small pieces and shards. Unconcerned about her own well-being, she climbed through and landed on a counter in the kitchen. She brushed herself off and made haste for the parlor. "I'm coming for you, you hear me, devil doll!" She entered the parlor, expecting to see Mary in the window, but she wasn't there.

Like a jolt of electricity, her body shivered as fear coursed through it. "Where did you go?" she asked, her head snapping back and forth as she looked for Mary. She spotted the bench and made her way there. She tossed open the lid but found it empty.

Footfalls sounded from upstairs.

"I hear you!" she spat as she ran from the parlor and up the stairs to the hall.

The whispers came and filled her mind with dark thoughts.

"Get out of my head!" she barked as she smacked her face hard, hoping that would stop the voices.

She first went to Lizzie's bedroom. The door was closed. She turned the knob and pushed it open. Cautiously she entered. The first place she looked was under the bed but found nothing, then to the dresser she went, and there too found nothing.

Knowing she didn't have much time, she exited the room and went to James' room. Like Lizzie's, she searched but didn't find Mary. From there her search went to the spare room. The second she entered, the wardrobe called to her. She went up to it, paused for a second to get her courage, then threw open the door, only to see that Mary wasn't there.

Footfalls sounded from above.

Is she in the attic? she asked herself.

Back in the hall she looked for a way to access the attic and saw a small door at the far end of the hall. She went to it and opened it up. There before her was a small set of stairs that led to a dimly lit space above.

The whispers came again.

"I know you're up there. You can't get away now," Sarah said then began her climb.

The attic was a large space, but the ceiling height was short, forcing Sarah to bend over. It was filled with crates. A small circular window at the front of the space brought in the only light, but it wasn't enough for her to see the corners, which sat dark and ominous.

"Where are you?" Sarah seethed.

The whispers grew louder and were all around her.

"Get out of my head," she wailed and put her hands to her ears, only to discover it did nothing to decrease the volume.

Louder the whispers got.

Distracted, Sarah pressed her eyes shut and shouted, "Get out of my head!"

As if obeying her command, the whispers stopped. A smile spanned her face as she found joy in that small victory. She opened her eyes, and there in front of her was Mary, a piece of wood with rusty nails in her hand.

Sarah turned to run, but it was too late. Mary struck her in the head with a fatal blow. She dropped to her knees. Mary struck again. Sarah cried one last time and fell to the floor dead.

A SHARD OF GLASS CUT JAMES' HAND AS HE SCOOPED up the scattered pieces of the window into the dustpan. He'd discovered the broken window upon returning home, and searched the house thoroughly but didn't find anyone or anything missing. He thought about contacting the police, but all they would do is write a report and move on. With this assumption, he'd set to cleaning it up and moving on with his day.

The blood from the shallow cut dripped onto the floor. "One problem after another," he grunted, putting down the dustpan and taking a rag to wipe up the blood. He leaned against the counter and thought about the past week and all the troubles he'd encountered since Mary came into the house. Could it really be that the doll was evil? Was that truly a possibility?

A knock tore him away from his thoughts. He walked to the door, opened it, and there stood Melody, her left hand still bandaged. "Hi, James."

"Melody, oh my, I wasn't expecting you. Did you send a note informing me you'd be stopping by and I missed it?" he asked, standing in the doorway, flummoxed by her surprise appearance.

"I was walking by and just stopped by. Call it an impulse," she replied with a nervous smile.

"Please come in," he offered.

"Is she here?"

"Oh, Lizzie, no, she's at school," he said.

"I don't want to upset her any more than I already have," she said and stepped across the threshold.

He escorted her to the parlor.

When she entered, she spotted Mary and paused. "Can I be honest about something?"

"Please do."

"Her doll, well, it's a bit off-putting, to say it nicely."

"It gives you a chill too?"

"More than a chill, I feel like it's looking at me, as if someone is really inside it," she said. She went to the chaise lounge and sat down.

He had similar feelings about the doll, but the instant he'd entertain it, he pushed the thoughts from his mind. "Can I get you something to drink?"

"I'm fine. I just wanted to come and talk. I thought we should."

"Yes, we should talk. I hope you received the flowers I sent and my note," James said, taking a seat across from her.

"I did, thank you," she replied and cleared her throat. "I care for you a lot, but after what occurred, I feel we cannot continue to see each other. The trauma it's caused your daughter is too much, but..."

"There's a but? I suppose that's good."

"But after some time we can revisit our decision. What I feel is best is for us to put some time in between what happened. Does that sound reasonable?"

"It does, and I can only keep saying I'm sorry for what happened. Lizzie is truly a sweet girl; however, I didn't realize how much the death of her mother troubled her. I owe it to her to guide her through this time and then, as you say, revisit our relationship."

"Good, I'm glad we've come to some agreement," she said and stood. Her body was tense, and her gut instincts were screaming for her to get out of the house as quickly as possible.

James stopped her at the door, took her hand into his, and said, "I love you, Melody."

"And I love you," she replied. Glancing down at his hand, she saw the cut. "Did you get cut too?" she quipped.

"I figured I wanted to feel your pain," he joked back.

Touching his face, she said, "I'll miss you, and please don't hesitate to send letters or the occasional bouquet."

He took her hand and kissed it. "Bye for now."

"Bye," she said, opened the door and raced out. She stopped for a brief moment on the sidewalk, spotted Lizzie on her way home, and went the opposite way.

After seeing her response, James stepped out and saw Lizzie coming. He waited until she arrived. "Hi, sweetheart, how was school?"

"Was that her?" Lizzie asked, her face scrunched.

"It was, but I can tell you that we're not going to

see each other, for now; we thought it best to take some time so that you can...get better."

"I'm not sick."

"Come on inside," he said and motioned for her to come.

Seeing his hand, Lizzie stopped and asked, "What happened?"

"I got cut by some glass."

Lizzie got a glimpse of Mary and asked, "Was she good today?"

"She's been right where you left her all day," James said.

"Good," Lizzie said, taking off her coat and running for the stairs.

James closed the door and called after her, "Aren't you going to get her?"

"No, I think I'll play with my other dolls today," Lizzie answered as she scaled the stairs and disappeared into her room.

7

BALTIMORE, MARYLAND
OCTOBER 21, 1887

"Daddy, Daddy!" Lizzie screamed.

Hearing the cries, James sprang from bed and sprinted to Lizzie's room. He entered to find her sitting up in bed, the blanket pulled up close and her finger pointing at debris on the floor. He looked more closely and saw it was her other dolls, but they had been torn to pieces.

"Mary did it. She was jealous!" Lizzie shouted, tears flowing down her cheeks.

He went to her side and comforted her. "Calm down."

After a few minutes of rocking her, Lizzie stopped crying. "She came in here and tore them apart. She's bad, real bad, Daddy."

He was speechless. How could a doll do this? Yet here he was, and there were the remnants of her other two dolls shredded on the floor.

"I'm scared," she wept.

"Want to come into my bed?" he asked.

She nodded.

He picked her up and carried her out of the room.

"I want her gone. Get rid of her, please."

"Okay," he said and placed her in the bed. He bent down and gave her a peck on the forehead. "It's been a long time since you called me daddy, I like that; it's nicer than father."

"Please get rid of her. I hate her."

"I'll go do that."

"No, not now, please not now," Lizzie said, grabbing hold of his arm.

"I can't get rid of her and still be here," he said.

"But what if she's in here?" Lizzie asked, her eyes as wide as saucers.

He carefully searched the room. "She's not here. I'm going to head down and find her. I suspect she's right where you left her in the parlor window."

"Hurry!" she cried.

He exited the room, closed the door behind him,

and made his way down the stairs, a candle in his hand. On the ground floor he went to the parlor, and there she was, sitting in the window. He let out a sigh. All he could think was Lizzie was sleep-walking or something. There was no other way of rationally explaining this and the other night. Maybe she was doing this and not knowing? He needed to get her help and quickly. But first, he would get rid of Mary. He snatched her from the window, took her into the kitchen, and put her in a sack. In the alley there was a crate; he'd leave her in there, tied up in the sack. Later on he'd ensure she was disposed of properly.

Torn about what to do with Lizzie, he decided he'd sleep on it then make a decision the next day.

THE WARM RAYS OF THE SUN PENETRATED THE window and hit James in the face. He opened his eyes, rolled onto his side, and found that Lizzie was sound asleep next to him. He placed his hand on her back and rubbed her gently. He loved her more than life itself and wanted to find a way to ease her pain as well as get her better.

By how bright the sun was, he could tell they were running late, and he didn't care. He rose, stretched and slid out of bed, ensuring he didn't wake Lizzie. He needed to use the bathroom and headed there.

As he passed Lizzie's room, he looked in and saw the torn and shredded dolls on the floor. His thoughts from the night before came: was she blacking out and sleepwalking? Did this all have to do with him having feelings for another woman and that triggered her?

Deep in thought, he reached the top of the stairs. Just before taking the first step, whispers sounded around him. He paused and looked back but saw nothing. He was familiar with the sound, as he'd heard it the other day, but quickly dismissed it then as his own imagination or a complication of fatigue or stress.

"Who's there?" he asked, even though he knew no one was there. He then recalled Sarah talking about hearing whispering, as well as Lizzie. He turned around and took a few steps. "Is someone there? Is that you, Mary?" he asked even though it felt odd to call out to a doll and expect it to reply.

The whispers grew louder.

To him it seemed like there was a dozen people around him, all talking at the same time and just low enough that he couldn't make out what they were saying.

Fear began to rise in him. He took a few more

steps and was now next to Lizzie's bedroom. He looked in the room again and this time saw something odd on the bed. Curious, he walked up to the doorway to get a better look.

In the center of the bed was a large dark spot, reddish in color. A drop suddenly hit the spot, forcing him to look up. There he discovered an even larger wet spot on the ceiling. He cleared the last couple of feet, dipped his fingers in the spot, and brought them close to his face. The second he was able to get a good look at it, he knew it was blood. Quickly he wiped it off, turned and headed out into the hall again.

Footsteps sounded behind him in the hall, followed by a door opening and more footsteps.

He spun around and saw the attic door was cracked open. Not waiting a second to confront who it was, he raced to the door, opened it and peered up the darkened steps. "Whoever is up there, come out now!"

The footsteps were now up in the attic.

"Come out now!" he hollered.

The footsteps stopped.

Not thinking things through, he ran up the stairs, his heart pounding with each step he cleared. At the top, he looked for whoever could be there, but saw no one. He took a few careful steps to his left and spotted the source of the blood. Cocking his head to get a better look, he saw a face. He wasn't sure if he was seeing things or that was the woman from the other night. With an abundance of caution, he approached, knelt and confirmed it was Sarah. He didn't need to check her vitals, as it was clear she was dead.

The heavy patter of footsteps sounded behind him. He turned around quickly and saw what he had doubted could be real. It was Mary and she was coming at him with a piece of wood, no doubt the weapon she had used against Sarah.

Mary swung the wood.

Using his instincts, he blocked the blow with his arm but didn't get away without injury as the nail penetrated.

With an uncanny strength, Mary pulled the board out and swung again.

James jumped out of the way. Terror overcame him, as he was having a difficult time coming to grips with what was attacking him.

Unrelenting, Mary came at him again but missed; however this time he grabbed the board, yanked it from her grip, and tossed it aside. This didn't stop Mary from her attack. She came at him and, with her wooden arms extended in front of her, shoved him.

James stumbled backwards, tripped over Sarah's

body, and went down, his head hitting the edge of a trunk. The blow to his head was enough to knock him out.

❦

T HE COMMOTION AND LOUD THUMP FROM THE attic woke Lizzie. She rolled onto her side and saw her father wasn't there. "Daddy!" she called out. She sat up, and it had to be at least midmorning, meaning she was late for school. "Daddy, where are you?"

Footfalls sounded outside the bedroom door.

Thinking it was her father, she said, "I'm late for school. Is it okay if I stay home today?"

No reply.

Lizzie could see a shadow coming from underneath the door. She knew someone was there.

"Daddy?"

The brass knob turned slowly.

Whispers came from the far side of the door, telling Lizzie it wasn't her father but Mary.

The door opened just a crack.

Unsure what to do, and frozen with fear, Lizzie sat, her knees drawn up close to her body. "Mary, is that you?"

With a forceful push, the door fully opened, and

there on the other side stood Mary, a knife in her hand.

For the first time, Lizzie was witnessing what she knew all along, that the doll was alive.

Mary took a single step; the whispers emanated throughout the room.

Lizzie screamed.

❦

THE FIRST THING JAMES SAW WHEN HE OPENED HIS eyes was the face of Sarah. He recoiled from the sight and scurried away.

Screams below echoed through the floorboards.

He sprang to his feet and ran. Down the narrow staircase he went and into the hall.

The screams continued and were coming from his bedroom, the door wide open.

He entered the room to see Lizzie on the bed, swinging a pillow.

Adjacent to the four-poster bed was Mary, very much alive, a knife clenched in her small wooden hand. Her head turned slowly and stared at him.

"Lizzie, I'm here. I'm going to stop her. You jump off the bed once I do, and run for help, get away from here."

"Daddy, I'm scared," Lizzie wailed, tears flowing down her cheeks.

Mary turned her attention back to Lizzie and, with a speed that seemed unnatural, jumped on the bed.

Lizzie screamed and swung the heavy down pillow. She connected with Mary and knocked her off the bed.

"Lizzie, come now!" James hollered as he advanced towards the bed.

"But—"

"Now!" James bellowed.

Pushing aside her fear, Lizzie ran and jumped from the bed and into James' arms. He turned to head to the door, but somehow Mary had gotten there before him. She raised the knife and came at him.

With Lizzie in his arms, he only had his legs to fight with. He cocked his right leg and kicked. The ball of his foot connected with Mary and knocked her back, but unfazed, she got to her feet again.

Realizing there wasn't a way for them to get through without him having the ability to fight Mary, he walked back and set Lizzie on the bed.

"Daddy, no, don't let go," Lizzie cried.

"I need to fight her," James said. "Pick up the pillow."

"Daddy, watch out!" Lizzie wailed, her eyes wide with fear.

James felt a stinging pain in his left thigh. He looked down and saw the six-inch knife was jutting out. He grunted, made a fist and smashed it against Mary's face. The doll went flying backwards and into a dresser. He grabbed the knife by the handle and pulled it out. Blood poured from the wound.

"Daddy!" Lizzie again cried.

Just as James looked up, he saw Mary was on her feet. The doll looked to the open door, then to him.

"Come on, attack me now!" James taunted, the knife now in his hand. He bent down slightly from the hip and readied for Mary's assault he assumed was coming.

Mary turned and ran out the open door, slamming it behind her.

Relief spread through him. He faced Lizzie and said, "She's gone, hopefully for good."

Lizzie wrapped her arms around his neck and climbed into his embrace. She put her face on his shoulder and sobbed.

"It'll be fine. We'll be fine, I swear it," he said and turned to look back at the door.

Minutes went by without a sound from Mary.

All James could think was she'd run away, but to where? Was she gone for good?

"I smell smoke," Lizzie said just as James too smelt it.

He limped to the door and opened it cautiously to see smoke billowing from Lizzie's bedroom. There was no time to wait. They had to make a run for it now or they'd no doubt perish in the flames. "Sweetheart, we need to go now. But can I get you to run? My left leg is in bad shape and—"

"I can run. Put me down," she said.

He put her down, looked at her deeply and said, "On the count of three, we're going to make a run for it. If something happens to me, don't stop, don't look back, just go, get out of the house. Do you understand me?"

"I won't leave you."

"If something happens to me, I need to know you won't stop running. Do this for me. Nod that you understand."

Lizzie nodded.

"One, two, three," he said and threw open the door.

The flames had migrated from Lizzie's bedroom and into the hall.

The two ran from the room and to the top of the stairs, avoiding the flames that had now begun to crawl up the walls.

Down the stairs Lizzie went, with James a few steps behind, as his leg was giving him trouble.

"Hurry, Daddy," she cried.

James felt when the arms latched onto his back and around his neck. He knew it was Mary and tried to throw her off but instead lost his balance and toppled down the stairs, landing at the bottom.

Seeing Mary atop her father, Lizzie screamed.

James went to get up, but he had now hurt his back. He turned his head towards Lizzie and hollered, "Leave, go!"

"No," Lizzie shot back. She looked around for something and spotted her father's cane. She ran to it, took it in her hands and came back.

Mary looked up at Lizzie.

Voices surrounded Lizzie. There were so many she couldn't understand what they were saying. "Leave my father alone!" Lizzie barked, cocked her arms back, and swung the cane like a baseball bat. She struck Mary perfectly in the side of the head and knocked her off. She reached out and took her father's hand.

Above them the fire was raging. It had now crept down the stairs, threatening them. The ceiling on the second floor was falling apart, with flaming chunks collapsing. It wouldn't be long before the roof came down on top of them.

James got to his feet with Lizzie's help. The two hobbled to the front door, but before they could open it, Mary attacked them again, this time focusing her assault on Lizzie.

Mary's hands wrapped around Lizzie's leg and began to crawl up.

Seeing what was happening, James grabbed Mary by the neck and pried her off. Filled with anger, he threw Mary into the flames that had consumed the base of the stairs.

Like dry kindling, Mary burst into flames. A single loud scream reverberated through the house.

Not wasting another second, Lizzie unlocked the door and opened it.

Fresh, cool air swept in.

They both stepped out into the chilly October air and took a deep breath. Passersby had gathered, and the sound of the fire department's siren rang from down the street.

They made it to the opposite side of the street before turning around to see their beloved home now fully engulfed in thick flames with black smoke billowing out.

Feeling relieved they had survived, James knelt down and wrapped his arms around Lizzie. "I'm sorry, I'm so sorry."

Lizzie pulled back and looked at him. "I told you she did it."

"I was wrong. Please forgive me."

"If it ever happens again, just please believe me," Lizzie said, her arms wrapped tighter around his torso.

"I'll believe you from now on, I promise."

"James!" Melody shouted from down the street. She ran and pushed her way through the gathering crowd.

The fire wagons appeared, and the men went to work on the fire, which now ravaged the house.

Melody reached James. She went to give him a hug but paused when she saw Lizzie. "Oh, um, what happened? Are you two okay?"

"We made it out alive," James said. "But I got a little hurt."

Looking down at James' leg, Melody gasped. "Oh dear, let's get you home and cleaned up."

"Not yet, I want to make sure that she gets..." James said before cutting himself off. He knew that telling Melody about Mary would only serve to alienate what was already a strained relationship.

"I'm confused. Is someone else in there?" Melody asked.

"No," James answered.

Cluing in, Lizzie said, "Just us."

Melody removed her gloves and touched James' face then Lizzie's. "I heard there was a fire, and I rushed down here, praying it wasn't your house, but I see I was wrong. The good thing is you two are safe."

"I need to sit," James said.

With Melody and Lizzie's help, James found a place to sit and watch his house and shop burn.

The firemen managed to stop the fire from spreading, but the house was a total loss. The roof caved in, destroying any evidence of Sarah's body. When the last fireman exited the ruins, he held something in his hands; it was wrapped in a blanket. He marched up to James and asked, "Was that your house?"

"Yes, sir, it was."

"And is this your daughter?"

"Yes," James answered.

"Then this is yours. I found it perfectly intact. It's a miracle it wasn't burned," he said and unwrapped the blanket.

Seeing it was Mary, Lizzie screamed and took cover behind James.

The fireman recoiled from her reaction. "This is your doll, isn't it?"

"Get it away from me," Lizzie cried.

"We don't want that doll, and I suggest you throw it away," James warned.

"Wasn't that your special doll, Mary?" Melody asked.

Lizzie didn't answer; she cowered behind James.

"Please, just dispose of the doll for us," James said.

"Very well, I'll make sure it finds the trash heap," the fireman said, turned and walked off.

Shocked that the doll hadn't a scratch or burn on it, James wanted nothing more than to get away from it and the house as fast as possible. "Can we go back to your place so I can get cleaned up?"

"Yes, of course."

With their help, James got to his feet. Together they hobbled down the street.

The fireman went to throw Mary in a heap of charred wood and debris but hesitated. He looked at her and said, "Why on earth would they throw you away?"

"Playing with dolls, are we?" another fireman laughed.

"They don't want it. I was thinking about taking her back to my niece Anna."

"Well, make up your mind. We've got work to do."

The fireman stood, his eyes fixed on Mary's. "Yep, I'll give ya to my sweet Anna. She'll give you a good home." He went back to the main wagon and put Mary in the back.

EPILOGUE

BALTIMORE, MARYLAND
NOVEMBER 13, 1887

"Well, that's the last thing we can salvage," James said as he watched the crew of men take a trunk from his shop and load it into a wagon.

"Father, is California really as nice as they say?" Lizzie asked.

"They call it the Golden State; has to have that name for a reason," James answered.

In the three weeks since their encounter with Mary, they had decided to move to San Diego. They didn't have family there, nor did they know anyone, but the move and the destination seemed like it was the right thing to do. Also they wanted to get far away from Baltimore, and San Diego fit that bill.

A carriage pulled up alongside James and Lizzie on the sidewalk. Melody stuck her head out the window and said, "Come, you two. We have a train to catch."

Besides the decision to make the move to San Diego, Melody and James had reconciled, with James asking her to marry, but only after Lizzie had given her approval. They didn't make it a big deal, having a local judge do the honors so they could leave Baltimore as husband and wife.

James opened the door of the carriage. "After you," he said and motioned with his hand for Lizzie to board.

Lizzie curtsied, giggling as she did it. She climbed on board, with James just behind her.

"To Penn Station," James hollered.

The carriage driver snapped the reins. The two horses lurched forward and pulled the carriage down the uneven brick street.

The three chatted and laughed all the way to the bustling station.

There they exited, with a porter coming to get their luggage.

"We're on the three o'clock, headed to St. Louis,"

James told the porter, a burly young man who stacked the luggage on a cart.

"Very well, sir, I'll have the luggage loaded for you," the man said.

James gave him a healthy tip.

They proceeded to the entrance.

Outside the swinging doors, people came and went, but a lone paperboy stood atop a wooden crate, selling the *Baltimore Sun* afternoon edition.

"Local family killed in fire. Survivor claims a doll was behind it!" the boy hollered. "Local family killed in fire. Survivor claims a doll was behind it!"

James and Lizzie both froze upon hearing the paperboy. They looked at each other, but neither said a word.

"Is everything okay with you two? It looks like you've seen a ghost or something," Melody said. She wasn't aware of the real cause of the fire that almost killed them, as James and Lizzie both had remained quiet about it and for good reason. Who would believe it?

James walked over to the paperboy, picked up the paper, and began to read.

The boy snatched it out of his hands and said, "Pay before you read."

Digging a coin from his vest pocket, James gave it to the boy. He quickly went back to reading and found the story. He read it until he came to the survivor's account, where she detailed the name of the doll was none other than Mary. Like before, fear rose in him. He folded the paper, tucked it under his arm, and said, "Let's go."

"Father, is it her?" Lizzie asked.

"James, you look ashen. Is everything okay? Did you know those people in the fire?" Melody asked.

He shook off the unexpected news and, not wanting to scare Melody nor discuss it, said, "I did know those people, very sad news, very sad."

She rubbed his shoulder. "I'm sorry."

"Father?" Lizzie growled, upset that she'd been ignored.

"Yes, Lizzie, it was her," James replied directly and firmly.

Lizzie's body tensed and her eyes darted around, half expecting to see Mary come out and attack her.

Seeing this was causing nothing but fear and confusion, James tossed the paper in a waste bin and put his arms around them both. "Come, family, let's get on the train. We've got a new home to go to."

"Yes, let's go to our new home," Melody said happily.

The three walked into the depot. James looked around as did Lizzie. Though they didn't expect Mary to pop out of any corner and attack them, they wouldn't feel truly safe until they could put the expanse of the continent between them and the evil doll that almost destroyed their lives.

THE END

———————

*THANK YOU FOR READING MY FIRST BOOK. I HOPE you enjoyed it. My Dad helped me with it, but the story is all mine and original. If you did like it, please leave me a review. Thank you. - Savannah

ABOUT THE AUTHORS

Savannah Hopf is a vibrant and fun student in elementary school. She loves animals, her family, friends, her dogs Stout & Bubbles and anything scary. When she's not in school, she can be found watching horror  movies with her Dad or playing Xbox. She lives with her family and an army of stuffed animals in San Diego, CA.

 G. Michael Hopf is a USA Today bestselling author of almost forty novels including the international bestselling post-apocalyptic series, THE NEW WORLD. He has made a prominent name for himself in both the post-apocalyptic and western

genres. To date he has sold over one million copies of his books worldwide and many of his works have been translated into German, French and Spanish.

He is the co-founder of BEYOND THE FRAY PUBLISHING and founder of DOOMSDAY PRESS . He's a veteran of the United States Marine Corps and lives with his family in San Diego, CA.

Made in the USA
Las Vegas, NV
14 June 2022